RISING

RISING

Sidura Ludwig

ILLUSTRATED BY

Sophia Vincent Guy

Candlewick Press

I rise with Ima in the early morning.

She places her special bowl
on the kitchen counter.
Yeast bubbles in the warm water.
My hot chocolate and her tea sit beside it,
steam from both our cups
rising.

I stir with a wooden spoon
flour,
then oil,
eggs,
sugar,
and a bit of salt.
Everything separate,
then mixed together.

We knead
the wet dough.
It sticks between our fingers.

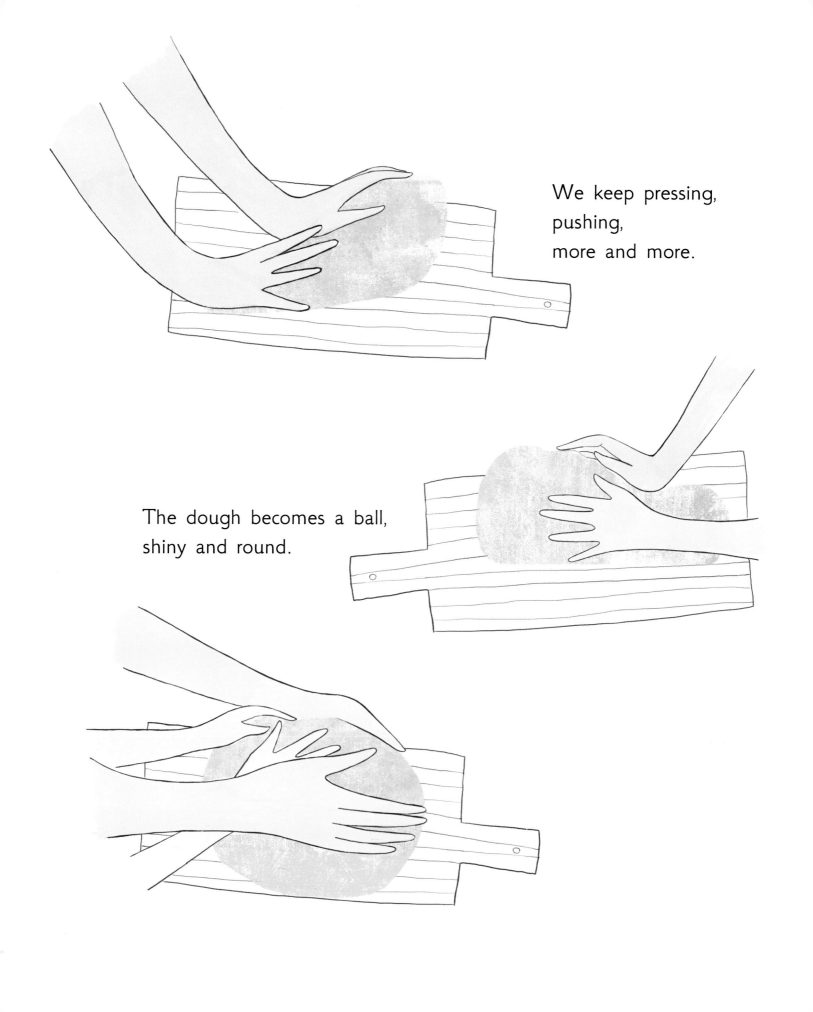

We keep pressing,
pushing,
more and more.

The dough becomes a ball,
shiny and round.

We tuck it under a towel,
like a baby
sleeping.

It rises
and we wait.
Ima says everything grows
in its own time.

Little bubbles
expand the dough
from the inside.
It swells
slowly,
like a deep breath.

We split the dough
into six parts,
roll them out like snakes,
and then we braid
six strands into each loaf of challah . . .

Just as six days of the week
become one
Shabbat.

Everything from the past week
comes to rest.

The challah rises again.
We tidy up
because Shabbat
is coming.

Our challah bakes,
rising with the heat.
A golden crust forms,
shining
like the sun through our window.

Our challah is done,
but too hot to touch.
Two loaves resting,
cooling,
waiting,
while we get ready
for our time
to rest.

Covered on the table
our challah sits.
We change our clothes.
Aba sets the plates.
Ima pours my grape juice.
We're ready to honor Shabbat,
as we do every week.

Our challah is ready
for *hamotzi lechem meen ha'aretz:*
our bread from the earth
that we made together,
that we will eat together.

We bless the candles.
We say kiddush.
We say hamotzi.
We say, *Thank you, Hashem,*
for so many blessings.

Our challah is for sharing,
for slicing and tearing.
We add a sprinkle of salt
for the times we've cried,
sometimes a dab of honey
for the sweet times to come.

I use my piece
to sop up the last bit
of soup.
It is my last bite before I'm too full.

Our challah is crumbs
on the table and floor.
I am too sleepy
to take myself to bed.
We are all ready to rest tonight—
each one of us—
all over the world . . .

until tomorrow
and the next day
and then the next,
when we come
together,
ready to rise
again.

AUTHOR'S NOTE

Challah is a special bread Jewish people eat every week for Shabbat. I make my own challah, and it's one of my most favorite times of the week. When I make challah, either Thursday night or early Friday morning, it means Shabbat is coming. Shabbat is a time when my family and I take a break from all of our work. We use no technology, we don't answer the phone, and we don't write or do any schoolwork. It's a time for us to be together without any distractions, to thank God for our many blessings, and to be with our community and friends around our table for joyous meals.

Challah is the center of those meals. I love being able to share something I've made from scratch with my friends and family. Because, above all else, challah is really meant for sharing.

Here's the recipe I use. Lori Grysman shared it with me. Now I will share it with you. When you make your challah, it will be like we are baking together.

CHALLAH

Yield: three medium loaves
Best made with an electric mixer using a dough hook,
but can also be done by hand.

Ingredients

2 cups warm water

2 tablespoons active dry yeast

1 tablespoon plus ½ cup sugar

6½ cups all-purpose flour, divided

½ cup canola oil (or other light oil such as
     vegetable or safflower)

1 extra-large egg (or 2 large eggs) plus 1 egg

1 tablespoon salt

2 tablespoons olive oil

Sesame seeds, poppy seeds, or everything
     bagel spice (optional)

Raw sugar (optional)

1. In a large mixing bowl, let the yeast dissolve in the water. Sprinkle the tablespoon of sugar over the top. Let the yeast bloom for five minutes.

2. Add 3½ cups of the flour, and mix on low until well combined.

3. Add the canola oil and extra-large egg, and mix well on low.

4. Add the ½ cup sugar and the salt, and mix well on low.

5. Add the remaining 3 cups of flour, one cup at a time, mixing well on low.

6. When all the flour is mixed in, increase the mixer speed to medium. Let the machine knead your dough until the dough forms a shiny ball. If your dough is wet, add more flour, ¼ cup at a time.

7. Brush on the olive oil to coat the dough. Cover the bowl and let the dough rise for two hours, or until it's doubled in size.

8. Divide the dough into three parts. Divide each part into three and roll into strands. Braid each set of three strands together, and place the braided challah loaves on a greased cookie sheet.

9. Preheat oven to 350°F. Let the dough rise again for 45 minutes.

10. Beat the remaining egg, and brush it onto each challah. Sprinkle on some sesame seeds, poppy seeds, or (my favorite) everything bagel spice and raw sugar.

11. Bake for 35–37 minutes, or until golden. Enjoy!

GLOSSARY OF HEBREW TERMS

Aba (AH-bah): Father

challah (HAH-lah, with a guttural *h* sound at the beginning): the special braided egg bread that Jewish people eat on Shabbat and most holidays

hamotzi (hah-MOH-tzee): the special blessing said before eating bread

hamotzi lechem meen ha'aretz (hah-MOH-tzee LEH-hem meen hah-AH-retz): bread from the earth; part of the hamotzi blessing

Hashem (hah-SHEM): literally "The Name"; one of the many ways Jewish people refer to God

Ima (EE-mah): Mother

kiddush (KEE-doosh): the blessing said over wine (and/or grape juice) for Shabbat and Jewish holidays

Shabbat (shah-BAHT): the Jewish Sabbath, from sundown Friday night until an hour after sundown Saturday evening

*For my children—Boaz, Dalya,
and Isaac
SL*

*To my two little bakers,
Aviv and Adele, and to little
bakers everywhere
SVG*

First edition 2024

Library of Congress Catalog Card Number pending
ISBN 978-1-5362-2549-5

24 25 26 27 28 29 CCP 10 9 8 7 6 5 4 3 2 1

Printed in Shenzhen, Guangdong, China

This book was typeset in GFS Neohellenic.
The illustrations were done in mixed media.

Candlewick Press
99 Dover Street
Somerville, Massachusetts 02144

www.candlewick.com